CW00864304

Coming alive

The Finest Pharaoh of All!

Stewart Ross

THE FINEST PHARAOH OF ALL!

PRINCESS HATSHEPSUT TAKES OVER EGYPT

STEWART ROSS

Illustrated by
SUE SHIELDS

EVANS BROTHERS LIMITED

TO THE READER

The Finest Pharaoh of All! is a story. It is based on history. The main events in the book really happened. But some of the details, such as what people said, are made up. I hope this makes the story easier to read. I also hope that *The Finest Pharaoh of All!* will get you interested in real history. When you have finished, perhaps you will want to find out more about Ancient Egypt and the time when Hatshepsut lived.

Stewart Ross

To the pupils of the Literacy Summer School, Tennyson High School, Mablethorpe.

Published by Evans Brothers Limited
2A Portman Mansions, Chiltern Street, London W1M 1LE

© copyright in the text Stewart Ross 1999
© copyright in the illustrations Sue Shields 1999

British Library Cataloguing in Publication Data
Ross, Stewart
The Finest Pharaoh of all! – (Coming alive)
1. Hatshepsut, Queen of Egypt – Juvenile literature
2. Pharaohs - Biography – Juvenile literature
3. Egypt - History - Eighteenth dynasty, ca. 1570-1320 B.C. – Juvenile literature
I. Title
932'.014'092

First published 1999
Printed in Spain by Gráficas Reunidas, S.A.
ISBN 0 237 51951 8

CONTENTS

THE STORY SO FAR...

THE EGYPTIAN EMPIRE

In 1493 BC, almost 3,500 years ago, Thutmose I became King of Egypt. In those days Egypt was a mighty civilisation. Its soldiers, builders and traders were the best in the world. Thutmose was a fine soldier who wished to make Egypt greater still, and he used his great skill to conquer many lands. In the south he defeated Karmah and carved a rock to mark Egypt's new boundary. In the east he defeated the Syrians and crossed the River Euphrates. Never before had the Egyptian Empire stretched so far.

THUTMOSE'S FAMILY

As was common in Ancient Egypt, Thutmose had more than one wife. It was also usual for members of the royal family to marry their own relatives. Thutmose's first and most important wife was his sister, Ashmose. The couple had three children. There were two boys and girl, named Hatshepsut. Thutmose's second wife was his aunt, Princess Moutnofrit. She had a son who, to honour his father, was also named Thutmose.

HATSHEPSUT

Hatshepsut's brothers died young. This worried King Thutmose, who wanted to make sure one of his family was King of Egypt when he died. So, towards the end of his life, he arranged a marriage between his two remaining children, Hatshepsut and her half-brother Thutmose. The king hoped they would get on, have lots of children, and keep the Thutmose family in power for years to come. But Hatshepsut and her half-brother did not get on ...

PORTRAIT GALLERY

Hatshepsut

Thutmose II

Ashmose

Thutmose I

Senenmut

Neferure

Karna

Amenhitop

General Ozah

Thutmose III

Amith

CHAPTER ONE

'HATSHEPSUT WILL BE KING'

Princess Hatshepsut was upset. It wasn't the flies, although they had been worse than ever this summer, even getting into her make-up jars. It wasn't the fact that her four-year-old daughter, Neferure, had been ill for weeks. It was what Hatshepsut saw at the military parade that had really upset her.

Princess Hatshepsut

General Ozah's army had just returned from the south, where they had won many victories. Hatshepsut had stood beside her elderly father, King Thutmose, as the troops marched past. The general looked magnificent. The captured treasure looked magnificent. But the ordinary soldiers were in a terrible state - thin, tired and many horribly wounded.

One man was so sick he collapsed right in front of the royal platform. When his wife ran out of the crowd to help him, a guard kicked her away. The soldier lay in the sun for hours, and when the ceremonies were over slaves carried away his dead body. The unnecessary cruelty made Hatshepsut's blood boil. But when she complained to her husband, he just laughed and called her a 'softie'.

Hatshepsut hated him. Not because of his ugly skin disease - he couldn't help that. No, she hated him because he was vicious and didn't have an original idea in his head. All he wanted was to be like his father. But the only thing the two men had in common was their name - Thutmose. Hatshepsut didn't reckon her husband was even worthy of that. She always called him 'Fritty' after his mother, the cowardly Moutnofrit.

Walking down the marble corridor towards her father's private rooms, Hatshepsut tried to cheer herself up by thinking of the good things in her life. As a respected royal princess, she was wealthy beyond most people's dreams. She was also beautiful and intelligent and knew how to read hieroglyphs as well as any scribe.

The trouble was, she was a woman. Egypt was run by men. When her father died, the wretched Fritty would become king and waste money and wage pointless wars. Hatshepsut could hardly bear thinking about it. If only she were in charge ...

'Welcome, Thunder-face!' smiled the king when his daughter entered. He was lying on cushions on a marble couch. A slave gently waved a large fan above his head. Hatshepsut

'Welcome, Thunder-face!'

bowed and gazed into her father's face. Although she didn't like his warlike ways, she respected his wisdom and his honesty. It made her sad to see how old he now looked. 'What do you mean, "Thunder-face"?' she asked, trying to sound surprised.

'You have no secrets from me,' he replied kindly. 'I can read your face like the carvings on a tomb wall. What are you worried about?'

King Thutmose I

Hatshepsut knelt beside him. 'Why have you sent for me, father?' she asked, ignoring his question. 'Are you unwell?'

Thutmose raised his hand. The fingers, once so strong and nimble, were scarecely more than reeds now. 'Listen carefully, dearest daughter,' he began, 'for I have called you here to tell you something of great importance.

'You are angry because you love our country and our people, and you fear what will happen when I am gone. But I promise you have nothing to be afraid of.'

'What?' blurted out Hatshepsut, 'Father, how can you say that when you know what a cruel boaster Fritty is?'

'Shh!' said Thutmose, slowly shaking his head. 'Answer this: What would you do if you were King of Egypt?'

Princess Hatshepsut

Hatshepsut had thought about this a thousand times. 'Change things!' she said eagerly. 'You have been a mighty king, father. Your armies went far and wide, and their victories made us rich. But now we need peace, time to enjoy our success. You know my dream? I want to send ships to God's Land, where the glorious King Mentuhotep sent ships 1,000 years ago. My ships will return with gold and spices and scents and ... '

'Just so!' interrupted the king with a smile. Then, to Hatshepsut's surprise, he lay back, closed his eyes, and spoke in a voice she had never heard before. 'My favourite child, you are right. Egypt needs peace. And therefore I

15

prophesy by the Great God Amon-Re that one day you will rule Egypt.' His voice sank to a whisper. 'Yes, when the gods are ready, Hatshepsut will be King of Egypt!'

CHAPTER TWO

PRINCE FRITTY

When she left her father's palace, Hatshepsut's mind was in such a whirl she could hardly think straight. She - a king! It was unheard of! Yet it had been prophesied. In the name of the great Amon-Re, too. So it was up to her to make the prophecy come true.

As soon as she got home, Hatshepsut took herself off to a private room to think things over. But no sooner had she kicked off her sandals and sat down, when Amith, her daughter's nurse, was shown in. Although Hatshepsut wanted to be alone, she always found time for Amith. The old slave, as wise as she was wrinkled, was one of the few people the princess felt she could really trust. She looked on her more as a mother than a servant.

Amith

Princess Hatshepsut

17

'Come in, Amith,' Hatshepsut called. 'How's little Neferure today? I hope you've got good news for me. I need it.'

Neferure

Amith smiled. 'Well yes, princess. The news is good. The doctors reckon your daughter is definitely on the mend. She ate two bowls of rice and fish, and asked for more! Shall I bring her to you?'

'Yes, do,' replied Hatshepsut. 'I shall take her to the temple to give thanks to the gods for making her better.' Amith moved towards the door. 'But before you go,' the princess went on, 'I need your advice on another matter. Come and sit on the floor beside me for a moment.'

Princess Hatshepsut

After she had dismissed her other slaves and checked to make sure there was no one about (Fritty was in a habit of paying slaves to spy on her), Hatshepsut told Amith about her father's prophecy.

'Well, what do you make of it?' she asked.

For a minute Amith said nothing. Then she looked Hatshepsut in the eye and asked slowly, 'And do you want to be king, Princess?'

Amith

'You know I do.'

'Then you probably will be. But don't hurry. First prove that you can rule as well as a man, and keep quiet about your dreams of peace. They may be seen as a sign of weakness.'

'And my husband? What shall I do about him? Have him killed?'

Amith looked surprised. 'You don't mean that, do you?'

Hatshepsut shook her head. 'No, of course not. But how can I be king while he's around?'

'You can't,' the nurse replied. 'But he's not a strong man and the jackal-headed god Anubis may well lead him off to the underworld before long. Just be patient, Princess. The gods always provide for those who wait. Now please may I go and fetch your daughter?'

As Amith was getting to her feet, the sound of angry voices came from the passage outside.

Seconds later, Prince Thutmose burst into the room.

Prince Thutmose

'So here you are, wife,' he sneered, 'plotting away with this old hag as usual. What is it this time? Are you going to poison me?'

Hatshepsut stood up and faced the prince. Her face was as hard as marble. 'These are my private rooms, husband. Please do not come barging in like that.'

Princess Hatshepsut

After looking around scornfully, the prince coughed and spat noisily onto the floor at Hatshepsut's feet. 'Yours? Ha! The old king will be dead before the end of the summer. Then I'll take over, and everything will be mine. And everyone

'These are my private rooms, husband.
Please do not come barging in like that.'

will do what I say. Even you, Princess hoity-toity Hatshepsut!'

Hatshepsut looked away. 'That's what you think, Fritty fool,' she muttered under her breath. 'But by Amon-Re! You've got a shock coming. I promise you.'

CHAPTER THREE

THE RUMOUR

The king did not die that summer, nor the summer after. He grew more frail and did not often leave his palace. But his mind was still sharp. He kept control of his kingdom through a network of loyal servants.

Chief among these servants was Senenmut the Scribe. He was a tall, lean man with bright eyes that gleamed like jewels from the south. The palace servants knew him as 'Senenmut the Wily', or the 'King's Ears', because he listened to

Senenmut

everything that was going on and reported it to his master at their daily meetings.

Hatshepsut was not slow to see Senenmut's importance. She gave him valuable presents of gold and silver, and invited him to be Neferure's tutor. After a while, he made a point of always calling on her after he had left the king. He was impressed with her intelligence and understanding.

Once, after one of their meetings, Senenmut said he though Hatshepsut would make a great king. When she said that was foolish talk because she was a woman and her husband would follow his father to the throne, Senenmut laughed and gave her a strange, sideways look.

'Your husband is only mortal,' he muttered.

Hatshepsut shivered. She knew what the words meant: in his roundabout way Senenmut was offering to help her kill Prince Thutmose so she could take over the kingdom. She made no reply. Although Senenmut was on her side, she knew she could never completely trust him. He was not known as 'the Wily' for nothing.

One warm spring day, as Hatshepsut and her slaves were bathing in a shallow pool of the Nile, one of her girls noticed a man approaching. As ordinary men were not allowed near the royal bathing place, two soldiers were sent to investigate. Five minutes later they returned looking rather embarrassed. Between them, dressed in his finest robes, stood Amenhitop, high priest of the temple of Amon-Re.

He was a tall, fidgety man who never took his hat off. If he did, one of his huge ears stuck out like the sail of a river boat and made people laugh. The high priest couldn't stand being laughed at.

'Most gracious, high and worthy Princess,' he twitched, looking at the sky because Hatshepsut did not have many clothes on, 'I beg forgiveness for interrupting you so rudely. But I have important news and must speak with you.'

'I'm all ears,' replied Hatshepsut without thinking. She glanced fiercely at her slave girls to

'Most gracious, high and worthy Princess, I beg
forgiveness for interrupting you so rudely.'

stop them giggling. 'Please, Great Amenhitop, tell me your news.'

The high priest flapped his hands at the gaggle of girls. 'What I have to say, princess, is rather secret. I think it might be best if these, er, maidens, did not ... '

Hatshepsut took him by the arm and led him to a quiet spot beneath a palm tree.

'No one will hear us now, sir. You may speak freely.'

For some time now, Amenhitop explained, a rumour had been growing about Hatshepsut's father. The princess looked surprised. She looked even more surprised when the priest said what the rumour was: King Thutmose was only Hatshepsut's father in name. Her real father was no less a person than the Great God Amon-Re himself!

The princess swallowed. 'And what does the king say?' she asked.

'He says with the gods all things are possible. You may indeed be the daughter of the Great Master, Amon-Re.'

Thinking fast, Hatshepsut asked, 'If this is true and my father is the Great Master, then what am I?'

Amenhitop lowered himself onto the sand before her. 'You, mighty Princess and Great Mistress, are a goddess.'

Hatshepsut lifted her head and looked out over the broad brown waters of the Nile. This, she thought, is the best news I have had for ages.

CHAPTER FOUR

'I HATE YOU, HATSHEPSUT!'

In the autumn old King Thutmose was called to the afterlife. His body was carefully preserved and shut away in its tomb with the things he would need for eternity, including his royal sceptre. Hatshepsut missed her father greatly and made a secret vow to raise a monument to him if she became king.

Fritty, now King Thutmose II, was officially in charge. Senenmut, Amenhitop and other important officials visited him regularly and pretended to do what he wanted. But in secret they saw Hatshepsut as their leader. After all, they told each other, she was a goddess. When the king gave an order, they immediately asked her what she thought. If she approved, they carried it out. If she did not, they made up an excuse to do nothing.

Senenmut

King Thutmose II

Amenhitop

Fritty, whose memory was dreadful, took a long time to see what was going on.

General Ozah

After Thutmose II had been king for a year, the people of Kush rebelled against their Egyptian lords. The king was furious and ordered General Ozah to take an army south and kill every male Kushite he could find. As soon as he left the royal palace, Ozah called on Hatshepsut and told her his orders.

The princess was furious. 'Does the king think he'll bring peace by killing?' she asked. 'No! You will not kill all the men and boys. You will use only enough force to put down the rebellion, then you will bring me the Kushite chief's eldest son. Understand?'

General Ozah did as Hatshepsut told him.

When he heard that the rebellion had been crushed, Thutmose II was delighted. He forgot to ask about the killing. But a few weeks later, as he was setting out to go hunting, he saw Hatshepsut and a young man standing before a temple dedicated to Sobek, the crocodile god. The king halted his chariot and got down.

'Who's that?' he frowned, pointing at the boy.

'His name is Karna,' the Princess replied coolly, 'and I'm telling him about the power of Sobek. Any objections?'

The king snorted and turned to get back into his chariot. Then he paused. 'He looks odd,' he said. 'Where does he come from?'

Thutmose II   Karna

For a second Hatshepsut hesitated. Her husband's eyes narrowed. 'I asked, Princess Stuck-up, where he comes from. Tell me.'

Hatshepsut looked straight at him. 'He is from the south,' she replied. 'He's a Kushite prince. I am showing him Egyptian ways so he can return home and teach them to his people. Then there will be no more war.'

Fritty looked as if he would burst into flames. Drawing his sword, he rushed at Karna.

Hatshepsut stepped into his path. 'To kill him, you must kill me first,' she said calmly. 'Surely you wouldn't kill a goddess, would you?' The soldiers and slaves murmured their agreement.

The king lowered his sword and slunk back to his chariot. 'I hate you, Hatshepsut!' he screamed as he rode away. 'D'you hear that? I hate you!'

When the king had gone, Senenmut sidled up. He had been standing nearby and had seen everything. 'Wonderful, Mighty Goddess!' he cooed. 'You have proved yourself as brave as a lion, a true king. What victories we shall have when you lead us!'

Hatshepsut shook her head. 'No, Senenmut. If I become king, I will be a king of peace. I will bring wealth, not war. I will send ships to the Land of the Gods and bring back riches.'

The scribe looked blank. 'Peace?' he repeated. 'Wealth? Trade?' Those are merchants' words, Princess, not a king's.'

'Then I shall be a merchant king.'

Hatshepsut   Senenmut

'I hate you, Hatshepsut!'

Senenmut bowed and turned away. 'Oh dear!' he muttered to himself. 'Whoever heard of a merchant king? That's not what we had in mind at all.'

A worried look came across Hatshepsut's face. If Senenmut turned against her, life could be very difficult indeed.

CHAPTER FIVE

THE BARGAIN

Now Neferure had grown into a healthy young girl, Hatshepsut liked nothing better than walking with her and Amith in the cool of the evening. Neferure was always full of questions, and one day she suddenly asked, 'Amith, why do people call mummy a king?'

Neferure.   Amith

The nurse sighed and looked at her mistress to answer. Hatshepsut took her daughter's hand. 'They call me a king, Neferure, because I tell them what to do.'

The girl thought for a minute. 'But doesn't the real king, Thutmose, do that?'

'Sort of, yes.'

'Then you're not really a king are you? And you never will be, because when Thutmose has gone from this life his son will be the next king.'

33

'Maybe,' replied Hatshepsut. 'But the gods sometimes have other plans. You see, I believe they want me to be king so I can bring peace to Egypt.'

At that moment, the princess noticed a figure standing behind some bushes to their left. When she called a guard to see who it was, the figure ran off. But Hatshepsut had seen enough to recognise him. It was Trith, Senenmut's secretary. He had clearly been spying on them. Hatshepsut decided to act - fast.

Trith

The meeting took place in the princess's private chamber. There were no slaves present and Hatshepsut herself checked to make sure they were not overheard. She came to the point the moment Senenmut arrived, before she had even offered him a cup of wine.

'This cannot go on, Scribe,' she began, sitting down on a small throne made specially for her.

Hatshepsut did not invite Senenmut to sit. He stood with his head on one side looking slightly confused. 'What cannot go on, Mighty Goddess?' he asked cautiously.

'You cannot go on spying on me, for a start.'

Senenmut looked uncomfortable but said nothing.

'Listen,' the Princess went on, 'I am probably the daughter of the Great God and it is prophesied that I shall be king. If the gods wish it, then it is our duty to make it happen. That includes you, Scribe.'

'Of course.'

'Right. It will be much easier if I have your help. You know more about the government of Egypt than any other man alive. You know every district, every governor, every priest, every soldier. You know, too, that I am popular and able. I will make a fine king. Together, we'll make Egypt greater than she has ever been before.'

Senenmut took a deep breath.

Senenmut   **Hatshepsut**

'Yes, Mighty Princess, I agree. But how will you make Egypt great?'

'I told you before - by bringing peace and riches. Don't you like the idea?'

'Maybe, but is it glorious?'

'What could be more glorious than a ship sailing home from the Land of the Gods laden with every luxury you can imagine? We would be the envy of the world.'

Senenmut frowned. 'But nothing like that has been done for a thousand years, Mighty Princess. Are you sure you can do it now?'

Hatshepsut laughed. 'Can I do it? I tell you, doubting Scribe, there will be not one but five treasure ships! Think of your share of the gold, jewels and spices! Isn't that better than any number of bloody victories?'

Senenmut nodded, then asked, 'And if the ships don't return?'

'They will. But I'll make a bargain with you. Stick by me until four months after the ships have left. If they have not returned by then, you will be free to find another king. But if you move before then, I'll have you buried alive! Agreed?'

'But how will you make Egypt great?'

'How can I deny someone who speaks with the power of a goddess? I agree.'

'Excellent!' said Hatshepsut, climbing down from her throne. 'And for once, Senenmut the Wily, I suggest you keep your word!'

CHAPTER SIX
'I SHALL BE YOUR KING!'

Although still a young man, King Thutmose II's health was failing fast. His wild behaviour only made it worse. He went off hunting for weeks, then returned home to a round of crazy parties. Once, dressed as a huge octopus, he got so drunk he fell into the Nile and had to be rescued by his soldiers. Occasionally, he got a guilty conscience and behaved normally for a while. But he soon got bored and went off hunting or partying again. Real power lay in the hands of Hatshepsut and Senenmut.

Hatshepsut   Senenmut

Hatshepsut was not the king's only wife. He had half-a-dozen others and one of them, a pretty little peasant girl, had born him a son. This boy, known as Little Thutmose because of his tiny size,

39

was the princess's greatest worry. He was growing up rough and fond of fighting, like his father. And as Neferure had pointed out, he was also next in line for the throne.

Hatshepsut's old friend Amenhitop, the twitchy high priest, solved the problem for her. She was worried, she told him, at the way Prince Little Thutmose was being brought up. He needed a wise, steadying influence. The next day Amenhitop went to the king and suggested that Prince Thutmose join the temple of Amon-Re as a trainee priest. Fritty was delighted to get his son out of the way, and the boy went to the temple to be educated in the ways of Amon-Re. Which included, of course, respect for his daughter, Hatshepsut.

Amenhitop

Nobody was quite sure exactly how King Thutmose II died. It happened while he was away in the south, hunting lions with General Ozah and Senenmut. One version of the story said that the king died after drinking too much wine. Another said he had a chariot accident. The only certain facts were that his body was brought home, preserved and

General Ozah

entombed. There was little ceremony, and few people mourned.

And so, with the goddess Princess Hatshepsut standing at his side, the ten-year-old Little Thutmose was crowned Thutmose III of Egypt. A week later he was officially engaged to be married to his step-mother's daughter, Neferure. Then he went back to his temple and she to her education. Hatshepsut's hour was approaching fast.

Thutmose III   Neferure

Nevertheless, Hatshepsut bided her time. She was now king in all but name, controlling every aspect of Egypt. Never before had a woman had such power. Strangely, however, there were few complaints. Thanks to her wise government, taxes were low and no men were dragged off to war. The merchants said times had never been so good. The land swelled with plenty, and even Senenmut had to admit that the people seemed happy.

After two years, on the advice of Amenhitop, Hatshepsut paid a visit to the oracle of Amon-Re at Karnak. She entered the temple alone and remained inside for over an hour. The huge crowd waiting outside grew restless.

Finally, Hatshepsut appeared. She was dressed in white and looked taller, more stately than before. She lifted her arms and the crowd fell silent. 'My people,' she began, 'I have a message from my father, the Great God Amon-Re, judge of all things.' She paused and looked around her. All her life she had waited for this moment. 'The god has declared that I, Hatshepsut, shall be your king!' After a moment's stunned silence, the crowd began chanting, 'Hatshepsut! Hatshepsut!' over and over again.

Hatshepsut

She lifted her arms and the crowd fell silent.

Hatshepsut then noticed someone standing at her side. It was Senenmut. 'Congratulations, Great King!' he hissed, smiling and waving at the crowd. 'But this is only step one, remember. Don't forget our bargain. Five ships laden with riches, or ... '

Hatshepsut didn't wait to hear any more. With a toss of her head, she turned and walked gracefully towards her chariot.

CHAPTER SEVEN

TO THE LAND OF THE GODS

Hatshepsut was crowned in a magnificent ceremony. She was dressed in royal robes and given all the signs of an ancient King of Egypt. She even put on the special royal false beard. Neferure said it made her look silly. 'So what?' her mother replied with a smile. 'Better to feel silly and be respected than feel fine and be laughed at.'

Hatshepsut

Later, Hatshepsut took on a special name from

Horus, the falcon-headed god. This made her a member of the Great House, or Pharaoh. It was a bold move, especially as Little Thutmose was still alive. But as her people admired her and she did the boy no harm, no one minded. Not for a while, anyway.

Horus

Hatshepsut put Senenmut in charge of the Royal Buildings. When she ordered a tomb for herself in the Valley of the Kings, he raised an eyebrow but said nothing. She also wanted the

45

temple to Amon-Re at Karnak completely rebuilt. Senenmut nodded and suggested it would look good decorated with stone pillars known as obelisks.

Senenmut   Hatshepsut

'Fine,' agreed Hatshepsut. 'But we don't want a row of measley needles.'

Senenmut looked alarmed. 'How big do you want them?' he asked.

'Let's say four obelisks, each thirty paces high?'

'Thirty paces! It can't be done!' spluttered Senenmut.

Hatshepsut folded her arms. 'Oh? You mean you can't manage it? Very well, I'll have to find another Buildings Manager, won't I?'

Senenmut gave in. He also agreed to begin a huge monument to Hatshepsut and her father, with the story of their reigns carved on the walls. She had always promised herself that she would honour her father in this way, and she was pleased to get the project started at last.

So far, so good, she thought when Senenmut had gone. Ten minutes later she was not so sure.

General Ozah was in a bad mood. He started complaining as soon as he entered the throne room.

Trying to keep his temper, he said that he didn't mind all this building and so on, but what was he supposed to do? Go fishing in the Nile? Egypt needed conquests and victories. He needed conquests and victories to make him rich. How could a soldier grow rich on peace?

General Ozah

Hatshepsut told him about the voyage to the Land of the Kings and the wealth it would bring. Ozah looked doubtful. 'It'll be very difficult to keep my officers happy with promises,' he said. 'They also want glory and spoils.' Hatshepsut promised him all the glory and spoils he wanted, but without fighting. Still Ozah was unsure, but he said he'd do his best to explain to his officers.

Ozah's visit worried Hatshepsut. Was he threatening her? Would he dare lead the army in rebellion? She needed to get her great voyage launched as quickly as possible.

Hatshepsut

Hatshepsut worked harder than she had ever done in her life. She arranged every detail of the voyage herself. She hired the best ships and chose the best rowers. Ramuse, the admiral in charge, was said to be the finest sailor in the world.

The five ships, each with a broad sail and thirty rowers, gathered at the port of Kosseir. They were loaded with everything southerners would like: fine jewellery, bright cloth, objects carefully crafted from copper and bronze, and jars of wine. Finally, water and food were taken on board, and all was ready.

Priests called on the gods to keep the ships safe. Trumpets blared. The rowers dipped their long oars into the water, and the great voyage began. Standing together, Hatshepsut and Neferure watched the ships slip slowly out of sight.

Neferure   Hatshepsut

Priests called on the gods to keep the ships safe.

'When do you think they'll be back?' the girl asked when the last sail had disappeared.

'Within four months,' replied Hatshepsut.

'How do you know?' asked Neferure.

Hatshepsut put an arm around her daughter's shoulders. 'Because they have to be, my love,' she replied. 'Our lives may depend on it.'

CHAPTER EIGHT

'THE FINEST PHARAOH OF ALL!'

The full moon came and went, and there was no news of the ships. Hatshepsut lay awake, worrying. If Admiral Ramuse brought back only a few mangy monkeys, her costly expedition would be a failure. Then General Ozah would demand war. Even worse, if the ships did not return within four months Senenmut might look for another king. Another king? That meant young Thutmose III. As soon as it was light, Hatshepsut sent for him.

Hatshepsut   Thutmose III

She was surprised how much more grown up the boy was. Despite his size, he had a noble, confident air. Quite unlike his father, Hatshepsut thought. Nevertheless, she was pleased to see that he still had great respect for her. He bowed to the floor when he entered and always addressed her as 'Goddess'. But something he said was less encouraging.

'Are you looking forward to the return of the Great Voyage?' she asked.

'Of course, Goddess,' he replied. 'It will solve many problems.'

Hatshepsut stiffened. 'What problems?'

Thutmose looked surprised. 'Why, if they do not return then I may become king before I am ready. That's what Senenmut the Scribe said, anyway.'

Thutmose III

'But I am pharaoh,' replied Hatshepsut quickly, 'so how can you be king?'

Thutmose looked away. 'I'm not sure,' he said quietly. 'But the scribe is full of strange ideas.'

When the boy had gone, Hatshepsut thought of having Senenmut put to death at once. But that would solve nothing, she realised. If Senenmut went, General Ozah would be left. And if she got rid of him, another then another would take his place. And so on.

No. Violence would not bring lasting peace. But the return of the treasure ships would. She went off to the temple of Amon-Re to make sacrifices for the success of the Great Voyage.

Another full moon passed, and still there was no news. Hatshepsut's servants kept a close eye on Senenmut and General Ozah. The scribe was working on his buildings, they said, and the general passed his time hunting. Neither was acting suspiciously.

Senenmut   **General Ozah**

At the time of the third full moon there were stories of storms at sea. Two days later, a spy reported that Senenmut and General Ozah had met at a remote spot in the desert. Hatshepsut did not arrest them. Instead, to keep Little Thutmose out of their hands, she ordered him to come and live in her palace. Finally, at the end of the following week, a messenger arrived from the coast ...

Senenmut was surveying Hatshepsut's tomb in the Valley of the Kings when a band of soldiers came to take him to the pharaoh. He was allowed to talk to no one. When he arrived, tired and dirty, he found Hatshepsut seated on her throne and General Ozah on his knees before her. The throne room was filled with a rich, mysterious smell.

'I have brought you here to teach you a lesson,' began Hatshepsut. The scribe's body was quivering with fear. 'You wanted a pharaoh to bring glory and wealth to Egypt. You said it could be done only through war. You were wrong.'

Senenmut　　　　**Hatshepsut**

As she spoke, slaves drew back silver curtains along one side of the room. The two men gasped. Stacked as high as the ceiling were ivory tusks, strange and beautiful skins, ebony, jars of perfumes, gold, silver, precious stones and frankincense.

'This,' smiled Hatshepsut, 'is just a little of what my ships have brought from the Land of the

As she spoke, slaves drew back silver curtains
along one side of the room.

Gods. We call it the Fruits of Peace. Some of it, of course, is for you.'

For a while Senenmut and Ozah were lost for words.

When the scribe finally spoke, his voice shook with emotion. 'How could I ever have doubted Hatshepsut, our glorious pharaoh and daughter of the mighty Amon-Re? Truly, mighty Goddess, you have shown Egypt a new way. You are indeed the finest pharaoh of all!'

WHAT HAPPENED NEXT?

KING FOR 20 YEARS

Hatshepsut ruled Egypt for almost 20 years. This was remarkable because when Thutmose III grew up he wanted a say in the government, and there was always a chance his supporters would rebel. But Hatshepsut managed to outwit them and keep herself in power. She was helped by a group of officials, including Senenmut, who remained loyal to her.

Hatshepsut continued to rule with great wisdom. She also went on with her building programme, and left more monuments and works of art than any other Egyptian queen. She avoided war, too. But at some time during her reign she put Thutmose in charge of her army. Of course, he wanted to use it. This was the beginning of the end.

WAS SHE MURDERED?

In 1458 BC the King of Kadesh, in Syria, led a huge revolt against the Egyptians. At this point, Hatshepsut died and Thutmose III took over.

Hatshepsut's death was very convenient for King Thutmose. He was longing to show his skill as a soldier, and now she was out of the way he was free to go to war. Because of this, some people think Thutmose brought about Hatshepsut's death.

THUTMOSE III

Thutmose defeated Egypt's enemies and went on to become a mighty warrior king. He waged seventeen different wars and set up a great empire. For some reason, he also ordered every mention of Hatshepsut to be removed. Wherever her name had been carved, it was changed to 'Thutmose'. Her tomb was destroyed and her mummy stolen. Senenmut's coffin was also destroyed, smashed into 1,200 pieces.

HOW DO WE KNOW?

RESEARCHING HATSHEPSUT

Researching Hatshepsut's reign is not easy. There are many children's books on Egypt, but they don't say a lot about Hatshepsut. There isn't much more in adult books, either. There are two reasons for this. First, because Hatshepsut and her family lived so long ago, there is very little left from those times. Second, it is difficult to discover exactly what she did because of Thutmose's efforts to wipe out all mention of her.

THE EVIDENCE

Like detectives, historians do their best to piece together the story from little bits of evidence. There is ancient picture writing (hieroglyphs) on rolls of early paper, known as papyrus. There are objects, such as jewellery and mummified bodies. (For example, from the mummy of Thutmose II we learn that he probably had a skin disease.) And, most famous of all, there are the wonderful stone monuments, such as the Pyramids, the Sphinx and the temple Senenmut built for Hatshepsut at Dayr al-Bahri.

THE ROSETTA STONE

The story of Hatshepsut's reign, including the great voyage, was carved on the walls of her temple. But for hundreds of years historians couldn't read the hieroglyphic writing. Then, in 1799, a Frenchman discovered an interesting stone near Rosetta in Egypt. The same thing was written on the stone in three languages: Greek, demotic (a form of Egyptian writing) and hieroglyphs. The Rosetta Stone was taken to the British Museum, London. Here, experts used it to work out the meaning of the hieroglyphs. Only then could historians begin to piece together the amazing story of Hatshepsut. Here is an example of what is written on the walls of Hatshepsut's temple. It tells of her ships leaving the Land of the Gods, which was also called Punt:

The ships were loaded up with the valuable cargo from the Land of Punt. There were precious, perfumed woods, frankincense, ebony and ivory ...

NEW WORDS

Afterlife Life after death.

Amon-Re A double god. Amon was a local god, shown as a human, a ram or a goose. Re was the eagle-headed sun god.

Ebony Hard, black wood.

Empire Foreign lands that a country controls.

Entomb Put in a tomb.

Eternity For ever and ever.

Hieroglyphs Picture writing used by the Ancient Egyptians.

Ivory Animal tusk or horn.

Kush The land to the south of Egypt.

Land of the Gods Modern-day Somalia. The Ancient Egyptians also knew it as Punt.

Loyal Faithful.

Mortal Capable of dying.

Obelisk A tall, pointed stone column.

Oracle Place where a god spoke to people, usually about the future.

Pharaoh The Ancient Egyptian royal family. It was also used to mean just the king.

Prophesy To tell the future.

Sacrifice Offering made to the gods.

Sceptre A rod carried by a king or queen.

Scribe A skilled writer.

Spoils Valuables stolen by victorious soldiers .

Trainee Someone learning a job.

TIME LINE

Beware! Historians rarely agree about exactly when things happened in Ancient Egypt!

BC

c. 2500 King Mentuhotep IV sends an expedition to the Land of the Gods.

1493 Thutmose I becomes king.

c. 1489 Little Thutmose born.

c. 1482 Thutmose I dies, Thutmose II becomes king.

1479 Thutmose II dies, Thutmose III (Little Thutmose) becomes king.

1478 Hatshepsut becomes king.

c. 1475 Hatshepsut sends ships to the Land of the Gods.

c. 1470 Hatshepsut's temple finished.

c. 1458 The King of Kadesh revolts against Egypt. Hatshepsut dies.

1426 Thutmose III dies.

AD

1799 Rosetta Stone discovered.

1822 Jean-François Champollion translates hieroglyphs.

1889 Mummy of Thutmose III discovered.

1894-6 Hatshepsut's temple discovered.

1962 Temple of Thutmose III discovered.